For Priya, my violinist daughter – P. M.

For Senka and Bisera – C.B.

First published in Great Britain in 2003 by
Frances Lincoln Limited, 4 Torriano Mews
Torriano Avenue, London NW5 2RZ
www.franceslincoln.com

British Library Cataloguing in Publication Data
available on request

ISBN 0-7112-2063-8

Set in Bembo

Printed in Singapore

9 8 7 6 5 4 3 2 1

Petar's Song

Pratima Mitchell

Illustrated by Caroline Binch

FRANCES LINCOLN

When Petar played his violin, everyone
listened. Whenever there was a celebration –
Christmas, Easter, sowing and harvest, weddings and
birthdays – Petar and the children went through
the village singing and dancing. Petar always
led the procession, drawing out melodies and
setting everyone's feet tapping to his jigs and polkas.

At Christmas time, Petar's father conducted the village choir.
His deep voice would ring out in the frosty night air: "Silent night!
Holy night!" When the children sang with him, their mouths
opened wide and caught the falling snowflakes which melted on
their tongues. Pine, candlewax and the rich
aroma of cinnamon cake scented the air.
It was a happy place.

One autumn evening, Petar was herding the cows home
from the high pasture and trying out a new tune on his fiddle.
Suddenly a loud explosion shattered the air. The cows and Petar
nearly jumped out of their skins.

Petar ran back up the hillside to see what was happening.
His heart turned a somersault as the rat-tat-tat of gunfire
bounced off neighbouring mountainsides.

He tried to round up the cows by playing their favourite
going-home tune, but it was drowned by the noise of church
bells crashing and jangling their terrible news – war had begun.

Long after Petar had gone to bed, he heard the murmur
of his parents' voices. They talked far into the night.

At dawn, Petar's father packed food and water.
He and Mother rolled up blankets and strapped them
on four rucksacks.

"Get ready, all of you. Go west." Father pointed to the other side of the mountains. "You'll be safe there. I'll follow as soon as I can." Petar, Gregor and Anna clung to him and wouldn't let go.

"Who will take care of you now?"
Petar whispered to his favourite cow.

As they set off up the hill, Father came running after them.
"Petar, you've forgotten your violin!" He gave him the case.
"Look after your mother, Gregor and Anna."
Then he went back to join the other men.

Night fell swiftly. They tried to stay invisible by keeping to the shadows. Spurts of red and orange flames in the valleys signalled houses on fire. Shells exploded in the distance. The wind howled and the forest crackled with menacing noises. They pressed on without stopping.

Three days later they crossed the border and reached a safe town. Their stomachs were empty and their feet were blistered and sore. The streets were full of other refugees looking for food and shelter. Children were begging for bread, and Petar saw a man snatch an apple from a market stall.

"Petar, play your violin," said Anna. "People will give you money, and we can buy food." But Petar couldn't play. His fingers felt stiff, like clothes pegs. There were no songs in his heart now.

Mother made a place to sleep in a doorway.
All night the snow fell. It was very cold.
Petar remembered how Father used to sing.

He remembered his friends saying, "Petar, play your violin!"
He shut his eyes and imagined they were all sitting in front
of the fire, roasting nuts. At last he fell asleep.

The next day, a kind man let them move into
his garden shed. He fetched beds, a table and a chair,
and made it warm and cosy. He even gave Mother
a job in the café. "I hope you'll be happy here," he
said. But how could they be happy without Father?

It was nearly Christmas. Anna and Gregor borrowed scissors and paper and glue to make cards to send to Father. But Petar didn't feel like making anything. What was there to celebrate?

The streets were deserted. Everyone was indoors cooking, wrapping presents and getting ready for Christmas Eve.

Petar marched – left, right, left, right. Where was Father now? Was he in danger? Was he marching down an icy road? Was he singing "Silent Night"?

Petar started to hum the tune to himself.

All of a sudden, a new melody came to Petar, a dancing rhythm, a tune to welcome the spring. He closed his eyes, searching for words that would fit. When he opened them, snowflakes were whirling down like tiny dancers. He tried out the tune in his head. Then he sang it out loud. Snowflakes floated into his open mouth and melted on his tongue.

He ran back to the garden shed. Where was it? Where had he put it?

There it was, in a basket of newly-laundered clothes. He opened the case and tenderly lifted out his violin. Then he picked up the bow and began to tune the strings.

Moments later, the sweetest of sounds reached the café. His little sister Anna cried, "Listen – Petar's playing again!"

Mother dried her hands. One by one, the customers left their food and came outside. Then they began to clap and snap their fingers.

Petar played all his favourite tunes,
one by one. Everyone linked arms and danced
the old jigs and polkas and waltzes. They laughed and hugged
each other. "Happy Christmas!" they cried.

Petar smiled. Suddenly he thought, "I can give Father something for Christmas! I'll give him my new song. I know we'll be together again, some day."

He hugged Mother, Gregor and Anna.

"Let's make a wish," he said. And just then, the words of his song came to him:

When swallows fly across the sun,
When Earth has woken up from sleep,
We'll sow the seed and beg the wind
To carry a song of peace.